Write on!
(☺)

Shannon
Anderson

MONSTER & DRAGON WRITE POEMS

Written by Shannon Anderson

Art by Sharon Vargo

To Mrs. Anderson's Poetry Club Kids. - SA

For my darling little monsters, dragons, and unicorns. —SV

MONSTER & DRAGON WRITE POEMS By Shannon Anderson
Published by Burnett Young Fiction
P.O. Box 1
Clarklake, MI 49234

ISBN Hardback: 978-1-64071-015-3
ISBN Paperback: 978-1-64071-016-0
ISBN eBook: 978-1-64071-017-7

Available in print and ebook from your local bookstore, online, or from the publisher at: www.BurnettYoungBooks.com

For more information on this book and the author, visit: http://www.shannonisteaching.com

Brought to you by the creative team at Burnett Young Books:
Meaghan Burnett & Cyle Young

Library of Congress Cataloging-in-Publication Data
Anderson, Shannon
Monster & Dragon Write A Poems / Shannon Anderson

Printed in the United States of America

Library Poetry Contest!
Submit your entries by Saturday at 8:00pm. Trophies for first and second place will be awarded!

“Oh my scales! What’s this?” Dragon asked.
“Well, obviously, it’s a poetry contest,” pointed Monster.
Dragon clapped, “I’m going to enter! I love writing poems!”

Dragon whipped out his writing notebook and scribbled down the details.

Monster found something to write on too.

"Monster, do you even know how to write a poem?"
"Um, yes. Of course. You just use a fancy pen and write fancy words," said Monster.

That afternoon, Dragon worked on a diamonte poem.

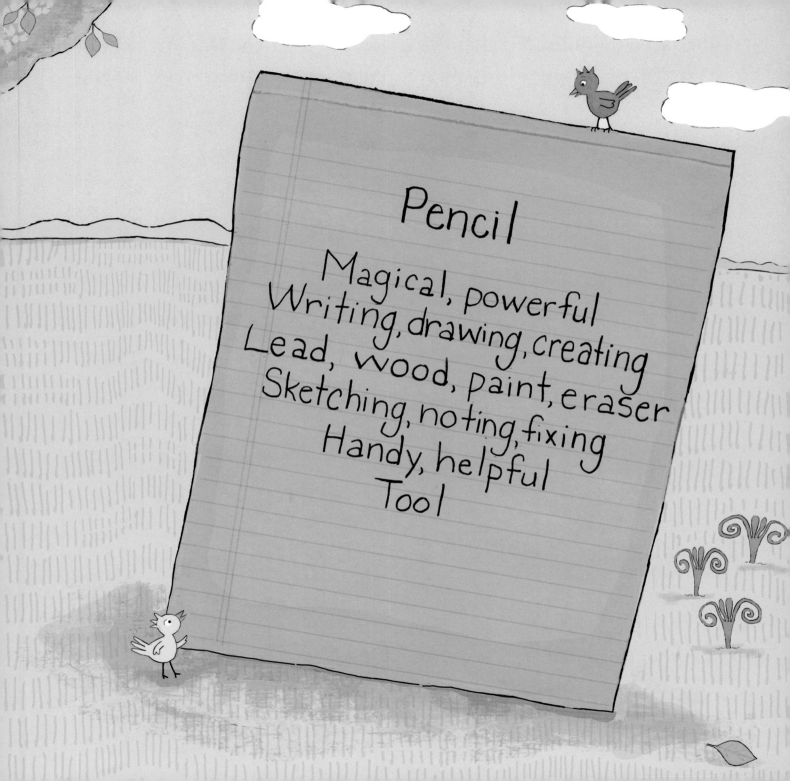

"What are you doing?" asked Monster, spying over Dragon's shoulder.
"I'm working on my poem for the contest."

"You're writing about a magical pencil?"
Monster snatched Dragon's pencil.

"Ooooh, Look at me!
I have a magical pencil!"

"Quit being silly, Monster.
Give me back my pencil.
I'm trying to write my poem."

Dragon grabbed back his pencil and went off to his cave to write in peace.
Monster sighed, "I guess I need to try to write my poem too."

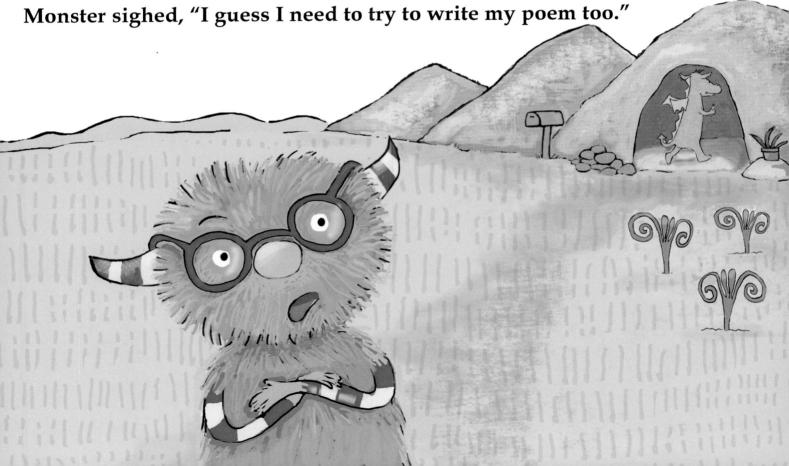

Monster didn't know
what kind of poem to write.
He needed to do some research.

Monster studied different kinds of poems.
He decided a haiku poem would be an easy one to try.

Monster was having so much fun writing his poem that he didn't see Dragon peeking in the window.

"Ha! That's the cheesiest poem I've ever seen! Good luck with that one!"

Dragon worked on a list poem next.

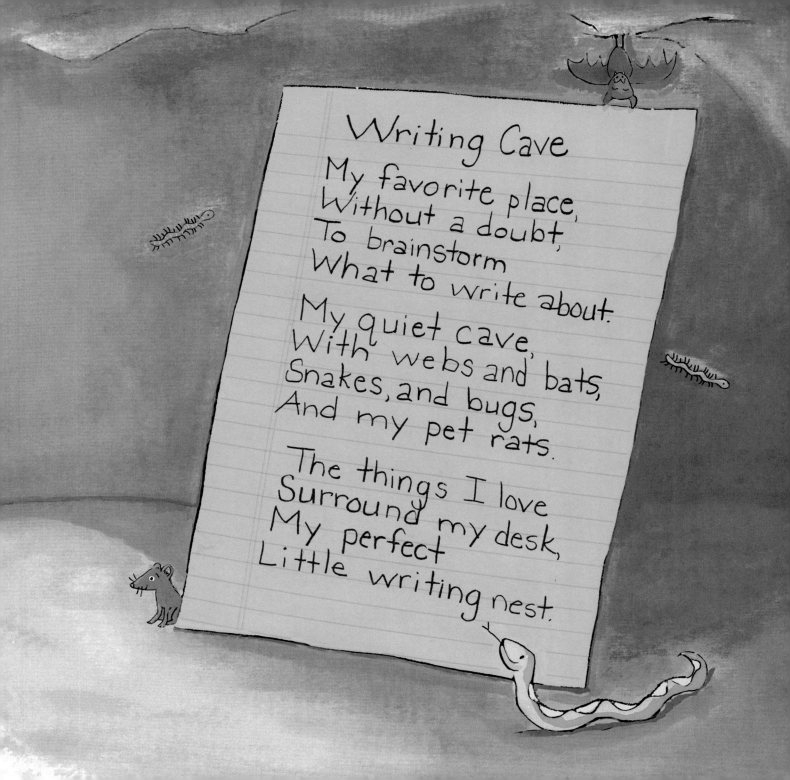

Monster decided he would try an acrostic poem.
He worked on it all morning.
And all afternoon.

And all evening.
And almost all night too.

Right before bedtime,
Monster finished his last line
and tucked it under his pillow.

Dragon got up bright and early. "Looks like today is the big day we turn in our poems! I better clear a space in my cave for my first place trophy!"

Monster held up his poem. "Maybe. Maybe not!
I'm pretty sure this is a good one."

Dragon took a closer look. He leaned in a little too close.
Monster's feather pen tickled his nose.

POETRY
by Monster

Paper and Pencil
Okay to be silly
Every word matters
Takes time
Rhymes sometimes
You create it

"Ah....Ah....Ahhh...Choooooooo!"

Monster's poem and feather plume went up in smoke.

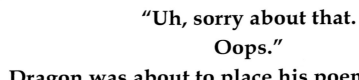

"Uh, sorry about that.
Oops."
Dragon was about to place his poems in the box,
when he saw a tear roll down Monster's cheek.

"No, Monster. Don't cry.
I didn't mean to destroy your poem."
Monster burst into a sobbing mess.

"Look, if you have to start over, I'll start over too."
"We can write in my cave."

They worked all morning.
And all afternoon.

And all evening.
And almost all night too.

Right before the deadline for the poetry contest,
Monster and Dragon dropped
their envelopes into the box.

Dragon
by Monster

There once was an impolite poet.
The problem was, he didn't know it.
He bragged all the time,
That he knew how to rhyme,
And took every chance he could show it.

Monster
By Dragon

There once was a writing beginner,
He worked hard from breakfast to dinner.
He wrote what he learned,
But his poem was burned,
And now, it cannot be the winner.

The day of the big announcement,
everyone gathered around the tree.
"Here is our moment, Monster."

Miss Llama announced, "The second place winner for the Library Poetry Contest is...

Unicorn, for her poem, Sunshine, Rainbows, and Lollipops!"

Monster whispered to Dragon, "I didn't see that coming."
"I know," said Dragon. "Maybe we tied for first place."

"And the first place winner is...

Bird, for her poem, Words Have Wings."

Dragon turned to Monster, "Well, that's a bummer."

"Wanna go get some ice-cream?"
suggested Monster.

Monster and Dragon started off, when they heard Miss Llama again.
"And the honorable mentions go to...

Dragon and Monster for their limericks about each other!"
Monster elbowed Dragon, "Honorable mention! I can live with that."

"I'm ok with being honorable too,"
smiled Dragon.

Forms Of Poetry YOU Can Try!

Acrostic - A poem with one word written vertically and each letter of the word becomes the beginning of a word or line about the word, written horizontally.

Haiku - a three line poem with five syllables in the first line, 7 syllables in the second line, and five syllables in the last line.

Diamonte - a poem in the shape of a diamond following this pattern for each line:

> **First line** - a noun
>
> **Second line** - two adjectives
>
> **Third line** - three verbs
>
> **Fourth line** - four nouns
>
> **Fifth line** - three verbs
>
> **Sixth line** - two adjectives
>
> **Seventh line** - a noun

List Poem - a poem with a short intro, a list pertaining to the topic, and a short conclusion.

Typically, there is rhyming and humor in this format.

Limerick - a five line poem that follows a rhythm and has a rhyming scheme of AABBA.